For Duncan and Charlie, with much love
VF

To Nika Sunajko
DM

Dora

Sam J. Butterbiggins
and Dandy the doodlebird

Prunella

Beezer

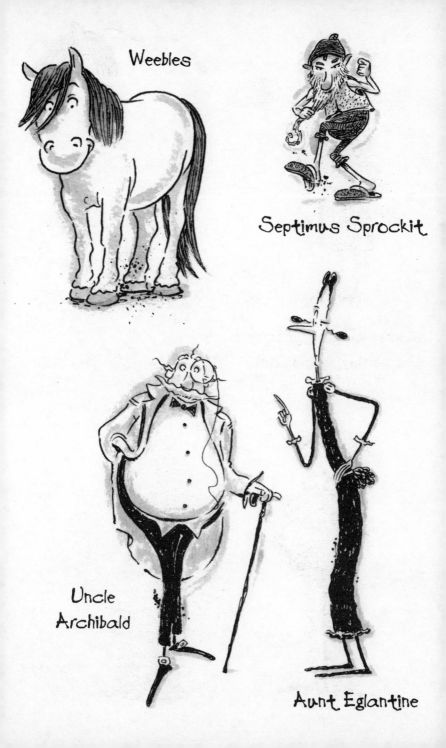

Weebles

Septimus Sprockit

Uncle
Archibald

Aunt Eglantine

AN EARLY
START

Sam's diary.
Very private.
Do not read.

Dear diary,

It's VERY early in the morning, but I'm much too excited to sleep.

Guess what? I've got a horse! My very own snow-white steed! A snow-white steed is EXACTLY what Very Noble Knights always ride, and I want to be a Very Noble Knight who does good deeds more than anything else in the world.

Sam closed his diary, and looked across his bedroom to where the doodlebird was fast asleep.

"What's the time, Dandy? Is it time to get up yet?"

The doodlebird woke with a jump. "AWK!" Then, making his point even more firmly, he tucked his head back under his wing and began to snore.

Sam sighed, and reached for his pen.

I'm on my way to being a knight. My True Companion (that's my cousin Prune) and I found an ancient scroll, and it tells us what to do. It's magic — the letters glow gold! And they get quite hot as well. Prune's looking after the scroll at the moment. I hope she's being really, really careful with it. We can't tell Aunt Egg what we're doing, because she doesn't like it AT ALL when Uncle Archibald tells stories about when he was young and was a Very Noble Knight. Aunt Egg is quite strict. I expect that's why Prune is sometimes annoying.

Sam stopped, and looked at what he had written. Was he being fair to Prune? He decided he was, and went on.

But, I don't mind staying here with Aunt Egg and Uncle Archibald while Mother and Father are away. I didn't like it when I first got to Mothscale Castle. The forest outside is really dark and gloomy, and the trees wave at me, and I can hear wolves — at least, I'm pretty sure they're wolves — howling all night long. But I like it much better now. If I wasn't here, I wouldn't have found the scroll, and I wouldn't have a True Companion, and I definitely wouldn't have my snow-white steed.

Thoughts of Dora, his big white horse, filled Sam's mind.

She wasn't far away, but if Sam could have had his wish he would have spent the night in the stables.

Aunt Egg, however, had squashed this idea flat. "Only horses live in stables," she had announced. "You, Sam, live in Mothscale Castle. You have a perfectly good bedroom, and I want you IN IT."

Sam had done as he was told. Only Prune ever argued with Aunt Egg. He had gone to bed, but it had been almost impossible to sleep. He had a horse! And Prune had her pony, Weebles! Surely it would be MUCH easier to do the rest of the tasks now, and then he would be a proper knight … He and Prune could ride out together, maybe even into the forest – and who knew what kind of adventures they would—

BANG!

Something hit Sam's
window, making him jump. Ink
spattered over his diary, and only a
wild dive saved the bottle from crashing
to the floor.

BANG!

Sam ran to the window, opened it and
looked out. In the
dimness of the early
morning light, he could
just see Prune waving at
him from the courtyard
far below. When she
saw his head the waving
turned to an imperious
beckoning and Sam gave
her a grin and a thumbs
up. Prune nodded, and
headed for the stables.

"Dandy!" Sam prodded the sleeping doodlebird. "Dandy! Prune's waiting for me!"

The doodlebird sighed. "Awk?"

"OK," Sam agreed. "I'll see you later." And, picking up his shoes, he hurried out of his bedroom.

FIRST CATCH
YOUR CASTLE

A few early birds were beginning to tune up for
the dawn chorus as Sam reached the stables,
but otherwise the world was very silent.
Prune popped out from one of
the stalls. "I thought you
were NEVER going
to get here," she said.
"Don't you want to
see what the scroll says?
I've been really good and
I haven't peeked. Not even
once."

Sam decided not to mention
that even if Prune had peeked, the scroll
wouldn't have told her anything. The next

task only appeared when the two of them were together.

"Go on, then," he said encouragingly. "Where is it?"

"In here." Prune led him into her pony's stall. "Weebles was guarding it for me. I didn't want Ma finding it … You know what she's like about knights and adventures."

Sam did know. The thought of Aunt Egg finding the scroll made him feel weak at the

knees. "Good thinking," he said.

"I'm VERY good at thinking." Prune was fishing about in the back of her pony's manger as she spoke. "It's under the hay somewhere ... Yes! Here it is!" She waved the ancient parchment in the air. "Let's unroll it together!"

The knight-in-training and his True Companion carefully unrolled the list of tasks. At first they could only read the introduction, which was always there.

Greetings to all who wish to be Truly Noble Knights. **H**erewith we offer you the tasks that should be accomplished, in order as hereby listed, that ye may succeed.

Prune groaned. "It's going to do it again," she said. "It's going to tell us to be patient!

17

It ALWAYS does that. Come on, scroll! We're
waiting! Give us the next task!"

"Give it time," Sam said. "It has to warm up
… Look! Here it comes!"

The two of them leant over the parchment
and slowly, letter by letter, a message appeared
in shining gold.

Task three. The knight-in-training and his
True Companion must find a goodly sword. Fear
not! It can be done! First catch your castle, and a
sword shall be yours.

18

"What?" Prune stared at the scroll. "Catch a castle? Whatever's it talking about?"

Sam shook his head. "I've no idea." Even as he spoke the golden letters began to fade, so he rolled up the parchment. "Where would we find a castle that needs catching?"

"There are loads of castles round here, but they all stay in the same place. At least, they always have up until now." Prune began to count on her fingers. "There's us here in Mothscale, and then there's Scratch Castle, and Grandmother isn't far away in Hollowfoot, and there's Puddlewink Castle where Ma's loopy cousins live. That's four. But I've never ever heard of any of them moving even an inch … Hey!" Her face lit up.

"What about looking in the forest? The trees
move around, so maybe a castle would as well?"

"Even if we do find one that moves, I still
don't see how we can catch a castle," Sam said.
He rubbed his ear, wondering if he should ask
about the wolves. Would Prune think
he was a scaredy cat? Aunt
Egg said there were no
such things, but Aunt Egg
had also said that there
were no walking trees,
and Sam had
seen one
with his
very own
eyes. And
there
was a
LOT of

howling every night …

Sam shook himself. He was a knight-in-training! Knights-in-training were NOT scaredy cats. "You could be right," he said. "Maybe we should look in the forest."

"Of course I'm right." Prune took the scroll from her cousin and tucked it carefully back under the hay. "And it'll be fun. You can ride Dora, and I'll ride darling Weebles!"

"Fantastic!" Sam beamed. "I'll go and find a saddle!"

Twenty minutes later, Sam finally rode Dora out into the courtyard, where Prune was waiting.

"Weebles and I were ready hours ago," she said accusingly. "You took AGES."

"I had to find something," Sam explained. He pointed to the coil of rope slung in front of his saddle. "I thought we might need this."

"Oh." Prune was unwilling to admit that this might be a good idea. "Well ... OK. But we'd better get going. Ma'll be up soon to feed her animals."

"What if we aren't back in time for breakfast?" Sam asked. "Won't Aunt Egg wonder where we are?"

Prune looked pleased with herself. "I left a note. I said we were going out for the day to study nature. Ma's very keen on nature. You know – bluebells and buttercups and all that

rubbish. If we bring back a few
flowers she'll be thrilled to bits."

Sam nodded, and together they rode away
from the sleeping castle. Sam was in a state
of huge excitement. He was, for the very first
time, riding his snow-white steed. The fact that
Dora kept stopping to help herself
to tempting tufts of grass didn't
bother him at all. She was his,
and that was what mattered.
He began to whistle happily,
until Prune glared at him.

"Sssssh!" she said. "We should be quiet!"

Sam gave one last whistle
to call for the doodlebird,
and as they reached
the edge of the forest
Dandy came flying
down to join them.

"AWK!" he said, and yawned.

"It's not that early," Sam told him. "And we need your help, Dandy – we've got to catch a castle! Could you fly over the trees and see what you can find?"

The doodlebird scratched his head. "AWK?"

"That's what the scroll said," Sam told him. "We've got to catch a castle, and then we'll find a goodly sword."

"AWK." The doodlebird still looked doubtful, but he stretched his wings and soared up into the sky.

"He's very useful," Prune said. "Where did you get him?"

Sam grinned. "He was a present from Mother and Father. He's meant to look after me, and remind me to clean my teeth and wash behind my ears and write my diary – stuff like that. But he's more of a friend, really."

Prune patted her pony's neck. "Like me and Weebles."

Sam was about to agree when Dora suddenly flung up her head, ears twitching.

Weebles did the same. Sam and Prune held their breath and listened.

At first, all they could hear were the usual noises of a forest: rustling leaves, birds twittering, the wind in the trees. But as the horse and pony slowly went on their way once more, Sam and Prune began to catch another, more unusual sound. There was a muttering and a mumbling and a grumbling, and as they wove in and out of the thick forest undergrowth it grew louder and louder and angrier and angrier.

"Battling beetles! Bothersome bottles! Blithering boots!"

SEPTIMUS
SPROCKIT

Neither Dora nor Weebles seemed afraid of
the shouting. Sam, looking left and right to see
where it was coming from, was not so sure. It
did sound VERY cross …

And then he saw a small hunched figure
dressed in red and tugging furiously at
his long white beard, which was
wedged by an axe into a fallen
tree. It looked as if he had been
there some time – the grass
was flattened
by his stamping
feet, and his face
was a remarkable
shade of purple.

He was much too angry to notice Sam and
Prune riding towards him; it was only when
Sam slid off Dora's back and came to stand in
front of him that he realised he was not alone.

"Ha!" he said. "Come to gawp? Come to
stare? Call me names, why don't you! Throw
sticks! Throw stones! Tell your friends!
Septimus Sprockit has made a fool of himself.
Try to cut myself some firewood, and what do
I do? Trap my beard!" And he went on pulling
and tugging.

Sam blinked. "Um ..." he said. "That is ...
Can I help you?"

"Help me?"
Septimus Sprockit
paused for
a moment
and stared
at Sam.

"Why in the name of Wittlespit would you do that? I don't give wishes, you know. No magic bottles, either. Nor porridge pots. Ran out of those years ago. Who are you, anyway? And who's that girl?"

"I'm Sam J. Butterbiggins, knight-in-training." Sam bowed. "And this is Prune, my True Companion."

The dwarf gave a sour laugh. "Knight-in-training? True Companion? Huh! I've met knights. Useless lot. They come trampling into our forest, and what do they do? Boast about their noble deeds and show off to us forest folk."

Prune rode Weebles closer. "If we're so useless," she said, "we'll just go. Come on, Sam!"

Sam hesitated. "We could try pulling the axe out," he suggested.

Septimus Sprockit snorted. "YOU? You're a mere BOY! If I can't pull it out – and let me tell you, I have the strength of ten of your beefy knights – you'll never do it."

"No." Sam was studying the axe. "But Dora could."

"Dora? Who's Dora?" The little man glanced at Prune. "Do you mean her? She's no good. Couldn't crack an egg!"

Sam didn't answer. He fetched the rope, and tied one end round the handle of the axe. The other he tied to Dora's saddle. "Come on, girl," he said. "You can do it!"

Dora, used to pulling a heavy wagon, made no complaint. She leant against the rope, and heaved …

and heaved …

and—

CRASH!

The axe flew
out of the fallen tree,
up in the air and into
the heart of a thorny
bramble bush.

"Hurrah!" Prune
cheered as Septimus
reeled backwards,
his beard flying
free. "Well done,
Dora!"

The dwarf glared
at her. "And who's
going to fetch my axe
back, may I ask? That's
the second I've lost.

Last time a knight came crashing through here he chucked my Double-Blade Ironhead into the back of beyond, and I've never found it. Meddle meddle meddle. That's all you humans ever do!"

Prune folded her arms and glared back at him. "You're a very rude little man," she told him. "You could at least say thank you!"

Septimus snorted. "What for? That was a perfectly good Single-Blade Coppershaft, and now it's stuck in the middle of a bush! Besides, I never thank anybody. Dwarves don't. I'll stake my beard you only helped me because you want something."

"We don't want anything." Prune stuck her nose in the air. "Well – not unless you can tell us where the moving castle is?"

"See?" Septimus glowered.

"You do want something! You lose my axe, then ask for a favour. Typical!"

Prune shrugged. "We'll find the castle for ourselves, then. Come on, Sam. Let's go."

"Just a minute," Sam said, and he began rolling up his rope. As he pulled the end free from the bush the Single Blade Coppershaft appeared, and the dwarf fell on it with a shout. Prune raised an eyebrow.

"Are you going to say thank you now?" she asked.

Septimus shook his head. "You don't listen, do you? I never say thank you!" And without another word he stamped his foot. A small door swung open in a nearby oak tree, and the dwarf hurried through. As the door closed, all sign of an opening vanished.

Sam whistled.

"Woooeeee! That's amazing!"

Prune frowned. "Huh! You did a really good deed, and that horrid little man didn't care at all."

BANG!

A window high up in the oak's trunk flew open, and the dwarf's head popped through. "Didn't say I didn't care, Miss Hoity Toity," he said. "If you

want to catch the castle you'd better
hurry. Down the path, first right at
the holly tree, then straight down the
hill to the river. If you're lucky, you'll
be in time. If not, then sucks to you!"
And once again he disappeared,
leaving a startled silence behind him.

"Oi! What did you done for
Septimus?" asked a deep growly
voice, out of nowhere. "He
never do nothing for
anyone, him! He be
super grumpy
dwarf!"

Sam and Prune
looked round, and
saw a large brown
bear leaning against
a pine tree. His

expression was friendly, but Sam couldn't help noticing the bear's long yellow teeth, and his heart skipped a beat.

Prune, on the other hand, seemed delighted. "Hello, Beezer! What are you doing here?"

The bear shrugged. "Going a walk."

Prune turned to Sam. "Sam – meet Beezer! He was one of Ma's lodgers for ages, weren't you, Beezer?" She giggled. "But Lady Gherkin never paid her bills, and Ma got really cross!"

Beezer nodded agreement. "Cross as buzzy wasps in jar!"

"And in the end, Ma told Lady G that if she didn't pay up she'd set Beezer free."

"Yuss!" The bear clapped his paws. "And my Lady G she say, bother that Beezer! He better go live in the forest! No cost money that way! And Beezer, he like forest lots and lots."

He nodded, then sighed
loudly. "But Beezer
not like Septimus. He
grumpy! Tell poor Beezer
go way, go back to lady and
be royal bear again, not forest
bear. Treads on poor Beezer's
toes. Pulls Beezer's nose – is very hurty! Tell
other dwarfies and gnomes and giants, 'No talk
to Beezer!' Beezer try and try make Septimus
like, but all no good. But Septimus help you! Is
miracle! What you do?"

"He'd caught his beard between his axe and
a fallen tree," Prune explained. "Dora – that's
Sam's horse – pulled the axe out."

The bear looked impressed. "Must be huge
strong."

"She is." Sam patted Dora's neck before
heaving himself up on to her broad back.

"But we need to be getting to the river, if you'll excuse us …"

"Yuss." The bear nodded. "Beezer come too."

"Oh … um … OK." Sam tried to sound pleased, although he was secretly wondering what the bear had in mind. Beezer kept looking at Dora in an admiring way – at least, Sam hoped it was admiration.

Prune heard the hesitation in his voice. "Stop worrying, Sam," she told him. "Beezer wouldn't hurt a fly, would you, Beezer?" As she spoke she shook her reins and set off down the narrow path at a brisk trot. "Come on."

As Beezer loped after Prune, Sam was relieved to find Dora was happy to follow the bear. Evidently she thought all was well, and Sam began to relax. Even when the path widened, and Beezer dropped back to lollop along beside them, the big white horse showed no sign of being anxious.

Sam felt very proud of his snow-white steed as they made their way down the hill. "She's wonderful," he told himself. "And soon we'll catch the castle, and then I'll get my sword!"

A SHORT CUT
— OR IS IT?

Sam was squinting through the trees when
Beezer stopped, and looked up at him.

"You want river? Beezer show quick way!
Fast fast faster!"

"But Septimus said we should go straight
down the path," Sam objected.

The bear shook his head.
"BAD dwarf! He no tell
you quick way, but
Beezer knows!"
"Prune!"
Sam called,
"Beezer says he
knows a short
cut to the river!

45

What do you think? Should we try it?"

Prune swung her pony round. "Of course we should! Beezer must know the forest like the back of his paw!"

"Follow close," Beezer said, and he set off down a narrow grassy track that led away from the main path.

Sam was almost certain he heard the bear chuckle, but he did his best not to feel suspicious – and at first, it did seem as if the track was heading the right way. Ten minutes later he was not so sure. They had twisted and turned so often that he had lost any sense of direction – the original narrow track had split several times, and still there was no sign of the river. Now they were travelling in single file along the very faintest of paths and Beezer was running faster and faster. Dora was forced to canter in order to keep up with him, and Sam could hear Weebles puffing hard behind.

"Beezer!" Prune shouted. "Are we nearly there?"

The bear didn't answer. He took yet another sharp right turn, then a left … and came to a halt. "Is here!" he announced.

Sam and Prune blinked in surprise. They were in a small glade surrounded by tall trees; it felt like the very heart of the forest.

"Where are we?" Prune demanded.

She looked at Beezer. "I thought you were showing us a short cut to the river!"

"That's right." Sam frowned. "What is this place?"

The bear caught at Dora's rein. "Not river. Beezer need help! Please? Huge strong Dora help Beezer?"

"Help you?" Sam tried not to panic. "But we really REALLY need to get to the river! I thought YOU were helping US!"

"We trusted you, Beezer!" Prune waved away a bee that was buzzing around her head. "What on earth are you playing at?"

Beezer pointed at the bee, and then at an ancient oak tree. High up between two branches was a deep hollow, and hundreds more bees were flying in and out in a steady stream.

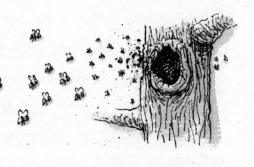

"Huge strong Dora pull tree down! Is honey tree – but too tall for Beezer! Dora pull down, then Beezer take Septimus Sprockit honey present, and Septimus like Beezer again!" The bear shook the rein. "Please!"

Sam stared at him, horrified. "Pull the tree down? But we haven't got time! We've got to catch the castle!"

"Just a minute." Prune was looking suspiciously at Beezer. "What did you do to Septimus? I thought he didn't like you because he was grumpy, but you just said, 'like Beezer AGAIN' ... did you upset him?"

Beezer's nose turned a glowing pink, and Sam guessed that he was blushing beneath his fur. "Was accident," the bear muttered. "Beezer had job in forest. Was working for Septimus, long time. Good work! But Septimus told Beezer to climb tree to fetch honey – he LOVE honey – and Beezer make little mistake. Dropped branch on head of dwarf. Didn't mean. Didn't mean at all."

"I see." Prune's expression was deeply disapproving, and Sam was suddenly reminded of Aunt Egg. "So you decided to trick us into coming here!"

"Pull tree down, then Beezer catch you castle!" Beezer began trying to pull Dora towards the tree. "Promise! Big true promise! Please help! PLEASE!"

An uncomfortable feeling was creeping over Sam. There was no doubt that the bear was very anxious and upset, so was he in need of a Noble Deed? Sam rubbed his ear while he tried to decide. Did Very Noble Knights do Noble Deeds for someone who hadn't exactly told the truth? Or did that make the deed not a noble one? And what if doing a Noble Deed meant you missed the chance to complete a task … a task you absolutely had to do if you were going to get to be a noble knight? It was very confusing.

And then, while Sam
tried to make up his
mind, Beezer let go of
Dora's rein, sat down, and
began to cry. Tears rolled
down his furry cheeks
and plopped on to the

ground, and he sobbed until he was shaking.

"Beezer very sad! Nobody talk to him.
Septimus tell everyone, BAD bear! Poor poor
Beezer!"

"Oh, bother!" Sam said. "Look here, Beezer
– crying's not going to help. And nor is trying
to trick people into helping you. Why didn't
you just ask us?"

Prune was still looking
remarkably like Aunt Egg. "I bet
you didn't tell Septimus you were
sorry, did you?"

52

The bear gave a mournful howl. "He very very VERY angry! Beezer ran!"

"Well, that's what I ..." Sam was about to say he would have done the same, but he caught Prune's steely eye and hastily changed his mind. He took a deep breath, and made his decision. In his mind he said goodbye to his precious sword. There was a more important deed to be done.

"Now, Beezer," he began. "Listen to me. I'm a knight-in-training, and Prune is my True Companion, and we do Noble Deeds. We'll help you get some honey, but you have to apologise to Septimus. Explain that dropping a branch on his head was an accident, and you're very sorry indeed and you won't ever do anything like—"

"Sam!" Prune was scowling ferociously. "Sam – we can't do good deeds for someone who tells big fat fibs!"

"Woooooooooooowlllll!" Beezer's wailing grew louder. "Woooooooooooooowlllllll!"

Sam shook his head at his cousin. "Yes we can. I'm sure he'll say he's sorry."

"That bear? Going to say he's sorry? Next thing it'll be raining pigs!"

The voice came from right behind Sam, and made him jump. He swung Dora round, and saw Septimus Sprockit staring at him from a window that had suddenly appeared in one of the larger beech trees. "No good for anything! Look at him! Great big

54

blubbering lump!" And with a CRASH, the window slammed shut, and both dwarf and window vanished.

"Oh dear," Sam said. "Septimus really doesn't like Beezer much, does he?"

"I told you—" Prune began, but she was interrupted. The doodlebird came flying in between the trees, squawking loudly with excitement.

"AWK! AWK AWK AWK!"

Prune leant forward. "What's he saying?"

"Yes!" Sam punched the air. "He says he's found the castle, and we might be in time to catch it!"

FOLLOW THE
DOODLEBIRD

"Hurrah!" Prune cheered, and she gave the doodlebird a thumbs up. "Let's go!"

There was an agonised wail from Beezer. "No go! Help poor Beezer!"

Sam looked at Dandy. "How much time have we got?"

The doodlebird shrugged. "Awk…"

"Um …" Sam scratched his head while he tried to think what to do. He wanted to help the bear – but if he was going to catch the castle, time was running out.

He turned to Beezer. "Dandy says we've got to hurry … so why don't you come with us?

And then we could help you afterwards."

Beezer wiped a tear off the end of his nose as he considered this suggestion. "Beezer help you, then you help Beezer?"

Prune snorted. "I don't know about that! You'll have to be REALLY helpful to make up for telling fibs!"

The bear looked sulky. "You bossy girl. Like Mrs Duchess! She bossy too."

He got to his feet. "Beezer don't want walk with bossy girls. Beezer go own way! Beezer no need bossinesses!"

He gave Prune a final glare, and stomped off in between the trees.

"Oh dear."

Sam looked after the departing bear with an anxious expression. "Do you think he'll be OK?"

"You're such a worry wart," Prune told him. "Of course he'll be OK. Come on – let's get going!"

"AWK!" The doodlebird flew to the end of the clearing and beckoned with a wing. "AWK!"

"We're coming," Sam said. He urged Dora into a lumbering trot, and Prune and Weebles followed close behind him.

At first the doodlebird led them along a narrow path, but it soon opened out and Prune was able to ride beside Sam. Gradually the trees grew further and further apart – and then, after a sudden turn, the river was in front of them.

"Wow!" Sam said as he stared at the rippling water. "Isn't it blue!"

He was right. The water was the clearest blue he had ever seen, and it sparkled in the sunshine. The river was wide, with tree-lined banks on either side, but there was an island in the middle. A very little island, covered with strangely shaped rocky crags and …

Sam gasped. It wasn't an island. Or, at least, not the kind of island he was used to. There was grass, and there were bushes, and rocks – but it was moving.

In fact it was floating … floating steadily down the river. And, as he went on staring, he realised that he wasn't looking at rocks at all. There were tumbled down walls, half a stone arch, the remains of a twisted tower … And it was all tiny.

"It's the castle!" Prune was actually smiling. "We've found it!"

"But it's so small!" Sam was open-mouthed in surprise. "It must have been built for very little people! Not even a rabbit could get through that arch!"

Prune shrugged. "It's still a castle. But how do we catch it?"

"We'll have to pull it in to the bank," Sam told her, and he was uncoiling the rope as he spoke. "Dandy – can you take one end of this and tie it to that tower?"

The doodlebird looked uneasy. "AWK?"

Sam nodded. "I see what you mean. You can't tie knots." He stared at the rope for a moment. "I know! I'll make a loop."

The doodlebird nodded enthusiastically, and a moment later was winging his way towards the island, the rope in his beak.

He dropped the loop over the remains of a pillar, and flew back as Sam encouraged Dora to pull. The little island swirled through the blue water towards them, and Prune jumped off Weebles to help bring the castle to the bank.

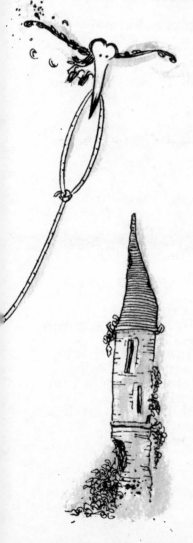

"I can't see a sword anywhere," she puffed. "Can you?"

Sam was too busy guiding Dora to answer, but as the island came nearer and nearer he could see how very old the ruined castle looked, and how the tiny stones were thickly covered in moss and lichen.

65

"Nearly here," Prune reported. "Just one more heave should do it. Ready? One – two – three – HEAVE!"

Dora, Sam and Prune heaved—

SNAP!

The rope broke. Dora lurched forward into a clump of nettles, Sam sat down on a thistle, and Prune, with a loud yell, fell on top of him. The floating island, released, began to circle away, trailing the frayed rope behind it.

"Oh NO!" Prune wailed as she and Sam disentangled themselves. "We're going to lose it!"

Sam struggled to his feet, rushed to the edge of the bank and – holding his nose –

jumped into the river. Splashing wildly he doggy-paddled towards the rope, but however fast he tried to swim it was always just out of reach.

"Go faster!" Prune yelled. "You've got to try harder, Sam! Go faster!"

But Sam couldn't go any faster. His clothes were weighing him down, and small waves slapped at his face, making it difficult for him to see. He made one final effort, but even as he stretched out for the frayed end, a swirl in the water carried it further away. He rubbed his eyes miserably and turned to swim back to the bank where his cousin was waiting.

"It's no good," he spluttered. "I can't catch it."

Then he saw the bushes behind Prune shake, and a moment later, a familiar furry figure came sprinting out of the forest. With a loud, "WEEEEEEE!" Beezer took a massive leap and hit the water with an enormous splash that all but drowned Sam. As the knight-in-training struggled back to the surface, coughing and spitting, he saw the bear swimming towards the island.

"YES!" Prune was dancing up and down. "Go, Beezer! Go!"

Sam hauled himself out beside her. "Where did he come from?" he asked.

"I don't know." Prune shook her head. "But look at him swimming! He's brilliant ... and yes! YES! Look! He's got the rope ... and now he's swimming back again! HURRAH! Hurrah for Beezer!"

HUNTING FOR
A SWORD

Towing the little island slowed Beezer down,
but there was no doubt that he was steadily
getting nearer. Watching him, Sam was trying
hard not to be jealous. But it wasn't easy.
"Prune NEVER says anything I do is any
good," he told himself, "and
now she's cheering madly
for Beezer – and a few
minutes ago she hated
him! It's not fair. She's
supposed to be my True
Companion, but all
she does is boss
me about. And
I did my best.

It's not my fault I can't swim very well ..."

He picked a piece of waterweed out of his hair, shivered, and turned to his cousin. "That water's really, really cold, you know," he said through chattering teeth.

"Run around a bit. You'll soon get warm." Prune was still gazing at Beezer in admiration. "But let's help Beezer out of the river first ... and we ought to tie up the island before it floats away again. Isn't it brilliant that he caught it?"

Sam, dripping wet, cold to the bone, and suffering from a strong sense of injustice, scowled at her. "I did try, you know."

Prune's eyes widened in surprise. "What ARE you talking about?"

"I tried my best to catch the castle," Sam said.

"Of course you did, stupid. You're a knight-

in-training, aren't you? You ALWAYS try your
best." Prune gave an exasperated sigh. "Why
do you need me to tell you that?"

Sam, confused, pushed a strand of wet
hair out of his eyes. "But you think Beezer's
brilliant, and not me."

"Don't be so silly!" Prune snapped. "You're
a knight-in-training, and I'm your True
Companion. We're a TEAM!" She banged Sam

on the back to make her point more clearly, almost knocking him into the river again. "I said Beezer was brilliant because he came back to help us." She gave Sam a sideways look. "I was beginning to think he was mean and horrible, and I don't like it when I'm wrong."

"No," Sam agreed. "You don't."

"But I nearly always AM right," Prune said firmly. "And I WAS right about Beezer being nice. Even if he did say I was bossy, which I'm not AT ALL. Come on – he's got to the bank!"

Sam, feeling much better, followed his True Companion to the edge of the river, where Beezer was heaving himself out of the water.

"Beezer catched castle," the bear said proudly. He gave the rope one final tug, and the little island came to rest in front of Sam and Prune, swaying gently.

"Where do you think the sword could be?" Sam asked as he peered at the overgrown turrets and walls.

Prune shook her head. "Could be anywhere."

"Go look!" Beezer encouraged them. "Beezer hold castle safe!"

"Thanks, Beezer!" Prune said. "Here goes!" And she jumped across the narrow gap, landing with a thump that sent the little island rocking wildly.

"Yes! Go find sword!" Beezer nodded, and sat down firmly on the end of the rope.

Sam hesitated. Prune obviously trusted the bear; he wasn't so certain. He looked across at Dora. She was grazing peacefully, Weebles at her side. He turned to the doodlebird.

"What do you thi—"

He was interrupted by an impatient shout from Prune. "Come ON!"

With a sigh, Sam stepped carefully off the bank, and the doodlebird flew up to the branch of a tree.

"AWK," he murmured as he settled down to watch. "AWK."

As Sam's back foot touched the ground he felt the island dip and wallow under his weight, and he stretched out his arms to balance himself.

"It's OK," Prune said. "It's a bit like being on a raft. Just don't move too fast. Can you see your sword anywhere?"

Sam cautiously peered around. There was ivy twisting and curling over the ruins, and a couple of small and stunted shrubs at the far side of the island, but no obvious sign of any nooks or crannies that might conceal a sword.

"Oh!" A glint of metal in the ivy at his feet had caught his eye. "What's this?" Bending down, he tugged at the tough wiry stems.

"Prune! There's something here!"

Prune made her way over to crouch down beside him, and together they pulled at the leathery leaves. "It's not a sword," she puffed. "It's got the wrong kind of handle ..."

"It's an axe," Sam said, and he pulled it out of the ground and stood up with it. "It's only an axe ..."

There was deep disappointment in his voice, but Prune ignored him and clutched at his arm. "What's happening?" she gasped. "Everything's gone green! SAM! What's going on?"

Sam couldn't speak. A shimmering green mist was floating in front of his eyes, and his ears were filled with the sound of silvery bells.

As the mist slowly cleared he saw hundreds of tiny figures staring up at him from the castle – a castle that was no longer in ruins. A small flag flew cheerily on the turret of the tower, and the broken arch was now a bridge across a sparkling blue moat. A troop of knights in shining armour came riding over, each mounted on a furry field vole. When they realised Sam had seen them they waved their needle-sized spears and cheered in shrill voices.

"Welcome to you and your True Companion! We welcome you to Elvish Island!"

Prune breathed, "Elves! Sam, we're seeing ELVES!"

Sam was too spellbound to answer. A thin flurry of notes from a trumpet had caught his attention, and a small group had appeared on the top of the tower, each figure no taller than his thumb. One, dressed all in speedwell blue, was wearing a crown of gold and silver and a minute page was holding up the edge of her gown.

"Sam J. Butterbiggins, knight-in-training," she called, in a voice like birdsong. "Princess Prunella, True Companion! You have saved us from the curse of iron, and we salute you! Iron fell on this island like a thunderbolt fifty years ago and cast us into darkness, for iron and the faery folk cannot live together. For fifty years we have sailed up and down this river, waiting to be released ... and now you, Sam J. Butterbiggins, have lifted the iron! You are our hero!"

Sam gulped. "Erm ... Thank you, your majesty ..." he said. "But ... but we didn't actually know what we were doing." He looked at the axe in his hands. "I think this must belong to Septimus Sprockit. He's a dwarf, you know."

The Queen of the Elves frowned. "We have nothing to do with dwarves." She tossed her head. "Brutish, earthy creatures, and lovers of iron. But now we must reward you!" And she clapped her hands.

"Sam," Prune breathed in his ear, "I think this is where  you get your goodly sword!" Sam was thinking exactly the same, his heart pitter-pattering in his chest.

"Here! Here is your reward!" the Queen

announced, and she held up something small that glittered in the sunshine. Very carefully, Sam knelt down and took the tiny object.

"Thank you," he said politely as he realised he had been given a silver coin. "Er ... thank you very much."

"And now ..." The Queen of the Elves was imperious. "Now – leave our island, human beings!" And she waved her hand. An unpleasant tingle ran up Sam's arm, and he gasped. Prune felt the same sharp shock and squealed loudly. Together, the knight-in-training, holding tightly to the axe, and his True Companion leapt for the shore, where Beezer was now fast asleep on the bank, the rope tied round his furry ankle.

"Quick!" Prune picked up the rope to undo the knot, but there was a tinkle of silver laughter from the elves. When she and Sam turned to look the island was already sailing away, the rope cut loose.

"Oh," Sam said. His disappointment was so intense he could think of nothing else to say.

Axes And Apologies

Prune tugged at Sam's sleeve. "What did the elf lady give you? It didn't look like a sword."

Sam opened his hand, and showed her the shining elvish coin. As he did so, it melted ... and all that was left was a drop of greenish water.

"Pooh," Prune said rudely. "That's not much of a thank-you present! You gave her back her castle! It was all ruins and rubbish!"

"Oh, well." Sam, doing his best to ignore the lump in his throat, heaved the axe on to his shoulder. "What shall we do now?" He looked down at the snoring Beezer.

"I suppose he'll want us to help him get his honey. I'd better wake him up." He bent down, and as he did so a small wiry hand grabbed his arm.

"Give me that axe!"

Startled, Sam did as he was told. Septimus Sprockit took the Double Blade Ironhead in his arms and cradled it as if it was a baby, crooning a little tuneless song.

"My own! My best! Have you come home at last?" He pulled off a twist of ivy still clinging to the handle, and peered up at Sam and Prune. "Where did you find it?"

"On the island," Sam told him.

"There were elves!" Prune gave an emphatic nod. "When Sam picked up the axe, a whole lot of elves appeared!"

"Elves?" Septimus sneered. "ELVES had my axe? Rubbish! Elves hate iron! They wouldn't touch it! Iron sends them loopy!"

"They said it arrived like a thunderbolt fifty years ago," Sam explained. "And it turned their castle into a ruin, and they all disappeared. At least, we couldn't see them. Not until I'd picked up the axe."

"Weeeeeeee!" Septimus gave a long whistle of astonishment, followed by a sly sideways look. "And did they thank you? Give you a

91

present? Gold? Wishes? Everlasting porridge?"

Sam shrugged. "A silver coin. But it melted as soon as we got back here to the bank."

"Ha!" The dwarf gave a shout of laughter. "Typical." He tucked the axe into his waistband, and patted it fondly. "All slip and slide and handfuls of mist, those elves. Not like us dwarves. Iron strong, we are. HUH!" He kicked open a door in a willow tree and vanished, slamming the door shut so hard he woke the sleeping bear.

"Erumph!" Beezer opened first one eye, then the other. "Dreamed I heard

Septimus." He rubbed his ears and nose, and squinted out at the empty river. "What? What happen?" He jumped to his feet in a panic. "No island! All gone! But Beezer has rope – where little island get to?"

Prune sighed. "It's floated away. It doesn't matter. We didn't find a goodly sword."

The bear rubbed his nose again. "Beezer sorry." He gave a mournful sigh. "Beezer not happy. So … we go find honey instead? Beezer must make Septimus Sprockit like him—"

CRASH!

The door in the willow tree burst open again, and the dwarf sprang out, his face as purple as when Sam and Prune first found him.

"Not happy? NOT HAPPY? And how do you think I felt when you dropped that branch on my head, you whinging whining pest of a

bear? When do you EVER get
anything right? I've no time for
you, no time—"

"Just a minute!" Sam, trembling on the
inside but doing his best to look bold and brave
on the outside, stepped in between Beezer and
the furious dwarf. Prune, scowling at Septimus,
came to stand beside him.

"You're wrong, Mr Sprockit." Sam tried to stop his voice wobbling. "If it hadn't been for Beezer you'd never have got your axe back. It was Beezer who swam out and caught the island ..." Sam's voice died away. The dwarf's face was rapidly changing colour, from purple to red, then back to purple, and finally red again.

"Oh, blistering bubbles and bristling bellows!" Septimus Sprockit stamped round in a circle, pulling at his beard. "Wittlespit help me! What's a dwarf to do?" Round and round he went, puffing out his cheeks and breathing harder and harder. Sam and Prune looked at him anxiously. Was he about to explode?

"Oh, bothersome bothersome BOTHERSOME bears!" The dwarf stopped, stuck out his chin and glared at Beezer. "Dwarves never say thank you. Never never never! But if they did, and I'm saying IF they did, which they don't, then Mr Septimus Sprockit would say it. And if you want your job back, Beezer Bear, then it's yours – but NO MORE CLIMBING TREES WHEN I'M UNDERNEATH! Understood?"

Beezer giggled as a delighted smile spread over his brown furry face. "Yes, Mr Sprockit! Beezer promise! Beezer do what Mr Sprockit says! Beezer be good faithful bear for ever and ever!"

"Then here's something for
you to do right now. Hop
down to the third room
on the right, and fetch
me the basket on the table." Septimus
sounded fierce, but Sam and Prune could
see a twinkle in his eye as he waved at the door
in the willow tree. Beezer squeezed through,
and Septimus leant against the tree trunk and
stared at Sam and Prune.

"So, Mr Knight-in-training and Miss
True Companion! First you rescue a stupid
old dwarf, then you set an island of pesky
elves free from the curse of iron. And then,
by thunder, you return a long-lost Double
Blade Ironhead to its rightful owner, let alone
making a dunderheaded bear extremely
happy. What, if I may make so bold as to ask,
do you plan to do next? Yet more good deeds?

If you're not careful you'll wear yourselves out!"

Sam and Prune looked at each other in astonishment, but before they could answer Beezer came hurrying back carrying a large

basket. "Here you are, Mr Sprockit!"

"Good." The dwarf took the basket and opened it. "Something for you, Miss True Companion," he said, and handed Prune a large bunch of wild flowers. "Twenty-seven different varieties. Your mother will be impressed. And for you, Mr Knight-in-training …" Septimus Sprockit bowed low to the wide-eyed Sam. "A goodly sword."

As they rode out of the forest Prune, who had been silent for a surprisingly long time, said, "Sam … I've been wondering. How did Septimus know we needed wild flowers?"

Sam, his gleaming silver sword safely tied to his saddle, shook his head. "I don't know."

The doodlebird, perched on Sam's shoulder, looked wise. "A<small>WK</small>."

"Really?" Sam turned back to look at the trees. "So he's got doors everywhere?"

"But we were talking about Ma in the stable," Prune objected. "Not in the forest."

The doodlebird shrugged. "A<small>WK</small>."

"The roof?" Sam said. "Oh, yes – it is a wooden roof …"

"Oh well." Prune patted Weebles' neck. "It's not worth worrying about. You've got your goodly sword, Sam. What do you think the scroll will say tomorrow?"

Sam, who was so happy he was almost beyond speech, smiled his widest smile. "Who knows? We did OK today, didn't we? In the end."

Prune grinned at him. "Elves and a dwarf and a bear ... and LOADS of good deeds!"

"Awk," said the doodlebird, and he stroked Sam's cheek with his wing. "Awk."

I don't think I'll ever be able to get to sleep tonight! I've got a True Companion, a snow-white steed AND a goodly sword! I'm really and truly on my way to being a Very Noble Knight.

I wonder what the scroll will tell us to do next? Prune's left it hidden in the stable. I think that's a very good place to hide it. Aunt Egg was a bit suspicious when we got back, but when she saw the flowers she was SO excited! Apparently one was a very rare Bluebellium something or other. She wants us to tell her where we found it, and go and get another. Prune thinks this will be a USEFUL EXCUSE if we want another day out.

A True Companion, a snow—white steed AND a goodly sword ...

Woooeeeee!

Join Sam and Prune
on their fourth quest!

KNIGHT
IN TRAINING

SPOTS, STRIPES
AND ZIGZAGS

Read on for a sneak peek ...

Hodder
Children's
Books

SALTY STEW

Dear Diary,

I've been sent to my room for being rude. Huh! I wasn't rude! At least, I didn't mean to be. All I did was say I didn't want any more stew, and when Aunt Egg asked WHY NOT? I explained it was just a little tiny bit too salty, and she said I was a Very Ungrateful Boy and sent me upstairs! Uncle Archibald winked at me when I passed his chair, so I think he agreed the stew was horrible. It was SO SALTY! I've been drinking LOADS of water, and I'm STILL thirsty.

It's REALLY annoying. Because the cook's gone off to see her poorly grandpa, Aunt Egg made me and Prune help in the kitchen ALL MORNING. We couldn't get to the stable*, so we couldn't read our magic scroll — and that means we still don't know what task we have to do today and it's getting later and later and later ...

(*Maybe we shouldn't have hidden the scroll under Weebles' hay. On the other hand, we can't risk Aunt Egg knowing what we're doing. She doesn't like anything to do with knights; she'd probably confiscate the scroll and use it for lighting the fire or something dreadful like that.)

How am I EVER going to be a Very Noble
Knight, and do Knightly Deeds, if Prune
and I can't do the next task? It's
AFTER LUNCH already, and I'm stuck
here in my room!! Prune's in hers, too.
She wouldn't even try the stew. She
said she'd be sick if she did, and Aunt
Egg went purple and told her she was a
Terrible Disappointment as a daughter.
Prune just skipped off —

"Psssssst!"

Sam jumped, and the doodlebird fell off his shoulder with a squawk as Prune came rushing into the room.

"Quick!" she said. "Pa's dozing in his study, and Ma's snoring in the drawing room, so we can get to the stable without them seeing us. I tiptoed right past Ma and she never even twitched!"

Sam looked anxious. Aunt Egg was Prune's mother, and Prune wasn't afraid of her ... but Sam found his aunt extremely scary, especially when she was in a rage. "What if she finds out we're not here?" he asked.

"Bah to that." Prune made a face. "She'll never come looking for you, because the stairs make her puff too much. Besides, she'll be going back to the kitchen to concoct some disgusting mess for supper as soon as she wakes up. She was using a cookery book as a blanket."

"Oh dear," Sam said, and Prune giggled.

"I know! She's HOPELESS at cooking!" She fished in her pocket and pulled out an elderly currant bun. "Here. I brought this for you – Pa has a secret stash tucked behind the chest in the hall. I've eaten three. I was STARVING!"

Sam ate the bun gratefully. "Thanks."

Prune looked pleased with herself. "I'm your True Companion, so I have to look after you, Mr Knight-in-training." She headed for the door. "Let's go – and don't make a sound!"

The knight-in-training and his True Companion tiptoed down the tower stairs, the doodlebird flying silently above them. The sound of steady snoring greeted them as they reached the wide hallway and, through the open drawing-room door, Sam saw his aunt slumped in an armchair clasping a large cookery book to her ample bosom.

"Careful!" Prune warned. Sam nodded, and they crept past, hardly daring to breathe.

Once they were on the other side of the doorway they began to run, heading down the long marble corridor towards the kitchen.

"We'll go out the back door!" Prune pointed to the left, and Sam gave her a silent thumbs-up. They rounded the corner at speed and—

CLANG! BANG! CLATTER!

Prune, Sam, Uncle Archibald and a rusty helmet collapsed in a heap.

GOBLINS

Beware – there are goblins living among us!

Within these pages lies a glimpse into their secret
world. But read quickly, and speak softly, in
case the goblins spot you ...

A riotous, laugh-out-loud funny series from the bestselling
author of HUGLESS DOUGLAS, David Melling.

www.hiddengoblins.co.uk